THE ECHO
of a
TROUBLED SOUL

Joy C. Agwu

First Published in 2013 by **The Manuscript Publisher**,
publishing solutions for the digital age -
www.TheManuscriptPublisher.com

ISBN: 978-0-9571157-6-7

A CIP Catalogue record for this book is available from the
British Library

Typesetting, page layout and cover design by:
DocumentsandManuscripts.com

Cover illustrations used courtesy of openclipart.org and
Wikimedia Commons. *African Phantasy* is a painting by James
Lesesne Wells (1902-1993).

All artwork has been used on the understanding that it is in the
public domain. This assessment is based on the most reliable
information available at the time of going to print.

Printed and bound in Ireland

THE ECHO OF A TROUBLED SOUL

DEDICATION

This book is dedicated to the almighty God who brought me this far, to Iris, Denis and Kerry O'Brien for their tremendous help and support, to my husband Edwin and my children - Victoria, Christian, Charity and Sandra - for their prayers.

ACKNOWLEDGEMENTS

I am grateful for the support and encouragement of Violet McKenna, Eva McKenna, Cecilia Kelliher, Pat Lavery, Nelie Kelliher, Miriam McGillicuddy, Gillian Wharton, Ann O'Sullivan, Elizabeth Powel, Bernadette Morkan, Bernadette Nash, Reverend Joe Hardy, Canon Warren, Ambassador Onochie B. Amobi, Josephine Neelon, Redmond Powell, Denise O'Sullivan, Hester Heals, Kerry Dunigan, Kitty Curtain and the staff members of staff of CDP Tralee, Co. Kerry.

CONTENTS

PREFACE

This story portrays a man at crossroads in his life and whose patience and self-control has been stretched to the limit. At this point, all garments of reasoning have been torn and the rules of engagement broken. It is about a man weighed down with bereavement following the sudden loss of all members of his nuclear family; except for his wife, who, in turn, has walked out of his life.

Consumed with grief, life no longer means anything to him. He is miserable, heartbroken, depressed, isolated and downcast. Like a dead man walking he goes in search of comfort and companionship and, unfortunately, finds them in alcohol. However this turns out to be the wrong step in the right direction.

Mother Luck shines on him when he meets a lonely boy who rescues him from his journey of self-destruction. The rainbow of hope glimmers in the sky when, after a long and painful search, he meets his long-lost daughter and a nephew. A new life is breathed into him; once more he feels the warmth of spiritual kindness and the benevolence of Mother Earth as he begins another journey of recovery.

CHAPTER ONE

Jane, Nora and the Old Man

Tom had a very happy family; only that his parents were poor. Growing up he had a brother and sister. His parents died when he was very young. Many years later Tom lost his brother, while his sister was missing since after her marriage to a strange man. Tom was left alone.

Every day, when he came back from work, he sat in front of his house watching the world go by. It was on one such day that he met a boy called Larry. Larry's experience was similar to his only that his father had died and his mother remarried and rejected him. They loved each other and Tom, after listening to Larry's story, took him into his house as his child. Larry is a very tall handsome, hard-working young man.

One day, when Larry went to work, Tom felt so sad that he went out and got drunk in order to forget his sorrows. He was so drunk that he started acting irrationally on his way home. It was Tom's irrational behaviour that brought Tom, Larry, Jane and Nora together.

Jane was well known in her neighbourhood, her school, Enugu state where she thought she came from, and beyond. She is a very tall, beautiful, smart and elegant looking girl, adored by her mates and loved by the woman she thought was her mother. Her popularity was mostly because of her beauty and performances in sports and education. She used to be the best in her class.

Many students wanted to be her friend but, because she was an only child, her mother never wanted her to have a friend; because Jane is very quiet and shy. One day Jane asked her mother: "Mom why is it that you do not want me to have a friend?"

Her mother said: "My daughter, it is because of who you are. You are very sensitive and shy, a very good and promising child. Moreover you are an unexpected gift, heaven sent. For these reasons I need to protect you always, because you are too young; you do not even know what friendship mean at this age and I do not want you to be upset ever in your life. If you have a friend, I am afraid that one day she may make you sad, and I cannot bear to see you sad.

"Again, if it is a bad friend, you will learn how to be bad and it is not what I want for you.

"When you grow up, you will have a friend, by then you would be able to differentiate between rights and wrongs; but for now, I need you by my side all the time, because you need to learn a lot from me so that you will grow up to be a responsible young lady, because you are all I have. Are you satisfied with my answer?" Jane's mother asked.

"Yes, mother I am satisfied. You are my friend, my best friend," Jane answered.

Jane's mother laughed, hugged Jane and they both went away.

Nora attended the same school as Jane. She was not an only child, her parents are very rich and she lives in the same neighbourhood with Jane.

One day the school closed earlier than usual and Jane's mother forgot that Jane was supposed to be picked up early. When Nora's parents came to collect her Nora saw Jane sitting under a tree. Nora was surprised to see Jane because she used to be one of the first to go home; as Jane's mother used to go at least ten minutes before closing time to pick her up. Nora is very good, friendly and talkative. And Jane plays with Nora. Their fellow students and even the teachers thought Jane and Nora were related.

Nora has always wanted Jane to come to her house, so she compelled her parents to take Jane home. Nora's mother told the school secretary to inform Jane's mother that they took Jane home. Later Jane's mother went to Nora's house to pick up Jane. Nora was only six years old then and Jane was six years old too. Nora asked Jane's mother whether Jane could be her friend; Jane's mother had no option than to say yes. Nora's parents convinced Jane's mother to let them bring Jane home from school so that she would not need to be leaving her work; that they could mind Jane in their house and bring her back in the evening if she wanted. Jane's mother agreed. That was how the two families became friends.

From then on Jane and Nora were very good friends. From childhood they grew up together in the same neighbourhood, went to the same schools and university. Nora's talkativeness was always the big problem between the two of them. One Saturday morning, during the rainy season when the two friends were coming back from the shop, Nora was talking too much and Jane was listening. She got so tired and fed up of listening that she did not know how to stop Nora. If she told her she was talking too much it would result into a long-lasting argument; and if she asked her to stop discussing other people's issues, it would result in a big fight.

Jane stood still while Nora, who had already discussed about three people including her next-door neighbour, started talking about the lady they had just met in the shop. She said the lady was a gold-digger. Jane interrupted: "Wait a minute, how come you know so much?"

Nora answered: "I know her very well. We worked in the same organization before."

Jane was angry. However, after a few minutes she came up with an idea and said to Nora: "You have been talking for a good while now and I have been listening to you; now it is my turn to talk while you listen."

"Okay," Nora answered.

Jane started by saying that, although she had no story to tell, she was going to recite a poem which she had learned when she was four years old. "This old poem is very good. It captured the attention of many people years ago; after hearing it my next-door neighbour told me that it was very inspirational, especially for those who believe that no-one is better than anyone else. Wait till you hear it, I'm sure that you will like it." She then recited the poem:

The Cultural Leadership in the Jungle and the Drums Of Africa

The world is like a marketplace,
Some are going to the market,
Some are coming back from the market.
That is how a market gets filled up with humans.
Give me my own, give me my own.
That is the noise you hear from the market.
Are you listening to the market drummers?
Are they drumming with your head?
Are you asking your neighbour what she came to buy?
Buy yours and go, because if she is not buying, she is selling.
Oh! Are you talking about the market councillors?
They are just doing their work. Why are you looking into your neighbour's bag?
She is either losing or gaining.
There are no two ways about it.
The world is full of joy and sorrow and so is a market.
Why are you asking your neighbour too many questions?
Do you want her to reveal the secrets of her life to you?
Oh! She is criticizing her neighbour, is she better than her?
Life and death depends on the power of the tongue.
The tongue is very good, it saves and it kills
And your tongue will either save or kill you.
If you want to be saved by your tongue, you are there to render justice,
If you want your tongue to destroy you, you are there to render justice.
But one thing is clear -
You will either choose to be destroyed by your tongue
Or choose to be saved by your tongue.
You must choose one, for sure; there is no middle ground,
You cannot hide; it is a tug of war.
If you think of the good, you must think of the bad,
If you think of the beauty, you must think of the ugly.
What of the past, the present and the future?
The mind is a wonderful thing to waste.

Nora asked Jane how come she knew the poem for so many years but had never cared to tell her about it before. Jane said that it was because she was waiting for the appropriate time and place to tell Nora about the poem. Nora asked her where she had learned the poem. She knew Jane did not learn it at school because they went to the same schools from childhood. Jane did not want to continue with the questions and answers so she simply said: "That poem is nothing but my brainchild, made up as a result of unfolding circumstances."

Nora reacted with fury and bewilderment. "Oh, how come you are only bearing that child now after a long period of incubation and many years of friendship and discussions with you? You never thought of bearing that child except now - or are you trying to demonstrate some sort of wisdom? Jane, I need an answer," Nora demanded.

Jane, sensing trouble, tried to calm her friend. "Nora can we please change the topic and move forward?" she said.

"Yes, we can move forward but, at the same time, we need to get to the bottom of this because, if we sideline the topic and bring up a new one, I don't think we will arrive at any meaningful conclusion and we'll create a vacuum which may bring strife between us," Nora responded.

They were about to enter the next level of argument when they saw a man behind them, singing in a very loud voice. It was an old man who was drunk. The old man came very close to Jane and Nora, paused for a while, looked around and told them that he had a question for them. Jane told him to ask any type of question, that they were ready to answer with pleasure. The old man asked: "Who is that soldier coming with you?"

They kept quiet. He asked the same question again and Nora said: "There is no soldier - it is only a statue of an old soldier."

He said: "That is not a statue. A warrior is coming to kill you and you are calling him a statue," and he shouted, "careless souls."

Little did they know that he was intoxicated with alcohol and, as if calling them 'careless' was not bad enough, he also called them 'drunks'. The old man was riding his bike and he got off it and followed the two friends, pushing his bike. Instead of continuing with the argument the two friends started planning how to escape from the old man. He continued raining verbal insults on the two friends. As the culture and respect for elder demands, they were quiet, but Nora, in characteristic manner, could not hold her peace. Rather than use her head, she turned to the old man and said: "Please, we want peace."

"Oh, there goes the tongue again," said Jane.

The man picked up a stone and threw it at her head. Jane could not help but laugh and the old fellow laughed as well.

Jane jokingly said to the old man: "We are getting close to the soldier, or warrior as you call him, and when we get to him we shall talk to him. I'm sure he is not going to kill us. However, if anything adverse happens, we will need your help. I think we are supposed to assist each other at all times, old one, what do you think?" asked Jane.

"Thank you, young lady, but make sure none of us cries or runs away because it is dangerous," said the old man.

"Okay," said Jane, "and nobody should talk too much either, because if a fish can shut its mouth it will never be a victim of the hook," she added.

"Yes," said the old man, "you have a point, young lady. I have taken note of that, but say that to your friend," suggested the old man.

Jane answered him saying: "Call her Nora, her name is Nora and she is my childhood friend."

"Okay, Nora, take note," said the old man.

Nora said: "All right, old one, not anymore. I have learned to shut my mouth because you taught me a bitter lesson not too long ago."

The old man laughed and said sorry to Nora, that he had not meant to hurt her.

"What is your name because we cannot continue to call you 'old one' when we know very well that you must have a name?" asked Nora.

The old man didn't tell them his name, instead he laughed and asked them whether they had been drinking. At that point they were a few yards away from the statute and they asked the old man to look at the statue, or the warrior. The old man quickly dropped his bike in the middle of the road and knelt down before the statue crying and asking the two friends to plead with the statue to not kill him, but to follow him and take his inheritance. Jane and Nora were baffled with the new development and attitude of the old man and they tried to persuade him to go home, but all to no avail. He stayed there for a long time and all efforts to convince him that it was an ordinary statue did not work.

The old man's behaviour caused a big traffic hold-up in the middle of the town, extending to more than three kilometres in all directions. The vehicles were not moving and the weather was very hot. The situation became so bad that a gentleman came out from his car, walked up to the old man, held him by the hand and told him to feel the statue. But the old man refused and continued crying. A large crowd gathered around him, pleading with him but he did not listen to them. He created a big scene, and the situation became so stressful that people started coming out of their vehicles to find out what was causing the traffic hold-up; because they thought there had been a fatal accident.

Someone pleaded with the old man to stop wasting their time and promised him a present if he went away from the middle of the road. The old man looked at him and said: "Poor fellow, you are blind, you did not take your time to look at me, you do not know how good looking I am." He went on, shouting: "Bloody people, they said I am drunk, but they are worse than me." Later, the situation became unbearable and some of the men told the old man to get out of the road or they would call the police. Still he refused to move. While they were still talking to him, a uniformed policeman, who had been called by Jane and Nora, appeared. The policeman made his way straight to the old man and told him to leave the road or he would end up going to jail for causing an obstruction; still the old man refused to move.

"I have respected you, yet you refuse to comply so you are under arrest," said the policeman. Although the young policeman knew the old man very well, he pretended not to because he was very unhappy to see him drunk once again, after all the advice and warnings he gave him before he went to work.

The old man told him to arrest the warrior first, that he was there before him and the policeman told the old man that he would arrest the warrior as soon as he left the road; still the old man refused to leave. The policeman then told him he was going to jail; he brought out his mobile phone on the pretext of calling for back-up. The old man, who had tasted the high-handedness of the police before, quickly stood up and pleaded with the policeman, saying that he wanted to urinate. Then a voice within the crowd told him to urinate on himself. In response to the voice from the crowd, the old man pretended to be pulling down his wears. But it was a gimmick; he took time to check where his bicycle was, grabbed it, jumped on it and took off down an alleyway, leaving the crowd and the policeman with their mouths agape and in a state of surprise.

The importance of all this, a voice from the crowd related, lies in the fact that the rat-race was temporarily brought to a halt, all by one drunken man and that, directly or indirectly, he created joy and released some of the tension within the crowd. There was peace at last, followed by laughter.

"We have to be foolish in order to be wise," said Jane.

"Poor fellow, he was in the world of his own," said Nora.

CHAPTER TWO

The One-Eared Old Man

Jane and Nora live in Maryland in the Ikeja suburb of Lagos. They live close to one another but not very close. Nora lives in a very big house while Jane lives in a two bedroom house.

Jane and Nora discussed the incident of the old man and laughed all the way home. Suddenly Nora paused and told Jane that she was very pleased with her poem and that she had learned a lot from it. They discussed a lot of things but when they got to the junction where they were to part ways, the two friends became sad because they did not feel like parting. They stood talking, but then Jane told Nora that she had to go because she had a lot of things to do at home. Nora suggested that it would be better if they lived together, but Jane said that was not possible because Nora was living with her parents, while Jane herself was living on her own. Nora told Jane that she was going to talk to her parents about moving in with her. When she got home and told her parents they granted her request and so, two weeks later, Nora moved in with Jane. They were very happy to live together.

"This is pretty good, at least I am free from the stress of having to call you whenever we have somewhere to go," said Nora.

"Me too," said Jane.

Sometime later, the two friends changed their jobs. Their new job locations were in the centre of the town, so they moved there to be close to work. Jane and Nora moved into staff quarters and the two of them were given a two-bedroom house each. However, they used Jane's house as their visitors' house and Nora's as their home.

One Saturday morning Jane and Nora were cleaning their house when, suddenly, a one-eared old man came knocking on their door. Jane opened the door and when she saw the old man she ran back and called Nora saying: "Come on Nora, a strange old man is at the door - come, hurry up, come and see him."

Nora hurried to the door. They both asked the old man what they could do for him but the old man did not answer and the two girls were very scared. The old man then asked them whether they remembered him, and they replied simultaneously, "No."

He told them not to be afraid, that they were his neighbours that he just felt he should say hello, and after saying those few words, the old man left.

One week later Jane and Nora were coming home late from work in the evening. At the entrance of their house they met the old man again.

"Good evening young ladies, how was work today?" asked the old man.

Jane and Nora said that the day's work had gone well and they asked him how he was.

"Good, thank you," said the old man.

Nora whispered to Jane that they should be on their way upstairs; that they should not allow the old man to keep them long. Jane pleaded with her to have a little patience.

That same old man was always stopping them whenever they were coming back from work. He asked whether they remembered who he was. Jane was thinking and kept quiet while Nora said: "No, tell us who you are."

"No, think," replied the old man.

Nora's patience was already wearing thin, so she said to Jane: "Not again, after a hard day's work."

The old man looked at Jane, laughed, and continued telling them stories about his being a soldier. Nora asked him: "What has the story got to do with us?"

The old man answered: "Everything."

Nora told him to keep the story until another time and the old man laughed and left. As soon as he was gone, Jane asked Nora what she thought about the old man.

"Nothing; or is there anything extraordinary about him?" asked Nora.

"Well, I do not think there is anything different in him. He is probably lonesome and simply wants a friend," said Jane.

"Oh, if that is the case, why don't you advise him to look for old men like himself, instead of coming here to disturb me with his stories which are of no interest to me?" said Nora, "Or, better still, you can go to his house and keep him company so that he will stop coming here."

"Nora, you do not understand, I'm trying to think," said Jane.

"Think about what? What manner of man he is? What he wants from us? Who he is? Where he comes from? What is his name? What does he do? Worse still, he said we are neighbours, yet he never told us which is his house or showed it to us," Nora complained in anger.

"Oh, yes, that is exactly what is bothering me," replied Jane, "I will try and find out more about him - what do you think?"

"Nothing, absolutely nothing, the only thing I am thinking about now is how to prepare the dinner." Nora angrily walked into the kitchen.

Jane sat down and pondered over the old man's statements. Nora came out to check whether Jane was still sitting down, only for Jane to start asking her whether she had taken a good look at the old man. Nora gave Jane a cup of tea saying: "Take a cup of tea - you are pretty much preoccupied with thoughts of the old man. The tea will give you enough energy to think, and maybe you can look for him and get all the information you need."

Jane went to the kitchen; Nora had already finished cooking dinner which she was then trying to serve. Nora said to Jane: "Get the table ready, Ms Old Man, please." Jane laughed and went to set the table.

As they were eating dinner Jane brought up the story of the old man once again, asking Nora whether she had noticed that he had only one ear.

"No," said Nora, "I did not notice. Has he really only one ear?" she asked.

"Yes, he has only one ear," Jane answered, adding: "You did not see it because your mouth was very busy."

"Oh, meaning that I was talking too much?" Nora asked Jane.

"Were you talking too much?" Jane asked, "Ah ha, you just told me. I only said your mouth was busy. Thank you anyway for telling me you talk too much," Jane said and laughed. Nora looked at her and told her that she needed a doctor.

After few minutes Nora said that if the old man had only one ear, that he must be a mysterious old man.

"I do not agree with you, but all I know is that as soon as I noticed that he had one ear, it reminded me of the story of the one-eared thief," said Jane.

"Oh, who knows? You might be right, he is the one-eared thief," said Nora.

Jane stood up and pulled Nora's hair and said: "I did not say that he is the one-eared thief, Madam."

Nora laughed and went to bed. Jane followed after her and told her that she wished they would never see the old man again.

"I regret the circumstances that made us to meet him," replied Nora.

They did not see the old man again for nearly a month. One Sunday afternoon, Jane and Nora came back from church service and the power was out. The temperature was about 48°C so everywhere was very hot. Their house was so hot they could not stay inside, despite the fact that they had left their windows open. They went outside. Directly opposite their house was a small market called *Fortune*. There was no buying and selling on Sundays so the girls went and sat down under one of the market shades. As they were talking, Jane said: "Oh my God, the weather is too hot."

A voice said: "Hotter than hell."

Nora said: "I wish rain would fall today."

The same voice from a moment earlier said: "Don't wish - let it come down."

Immediately the two friends stood up and looked around, but they did not see anyone. Beside them was an iron barricade. They walked across it and saw an old man sitting down on a bench with a book titled, *The Bastards*. The old man raised his face and, behold, it was the same old fellow they thought they would never see again.

Nora shouted: "Goodness me, not again."

"Keep quiet, Nora," said Jane.

"She can never change," said the old man;

'Besides, do you now remember who I am?" he asked.

"No," they said.

"I do not know what you mean by that because you never told us who you are, old one," said Nora.

"Easy, Nora," Jane said.

"If a fish can shut its mouth it will never be a victim of the hook," said the old man.

"Ah!" cried Jane, "where did you get this statement, old one?" Jane was anxious to know.

The old man smiled and said: "From you, of course."

"You mean from me or from Nora?" asked Jane.

The man laughed and asked them whether they remembered when they went to call the police to force an old man out off the main road, when he was pleading with a statue not to kill him.

"Yes," they said.

"But that was a long time ago," said Jane.

"Were you there?" Nora asked the old man.

"Well, that old man is here," he said with a big smile on his face.

"Where is he?" Nora asked.

"It is me, I am the old man," he replied.

The two friends were surprised. Then Nora asked the old man about what happened to his left ear.

He replied: "I knew that you would be the one that would ask - do you always talk this much, Nora?"

Nora kept quiet.

The old man turned to Jane and said: "Are you always this shy, Jane?"

Jane kept quiet too.

The old man asked them to sit down with him. They sat down and Nora took the book from him and read the summary at the back of it. Then she gave it to Jane who read it also. They looked at one another and Nora said: "Oh, what an interesting story. Can you tell us the full story?"

"I wonder whether your friend would like to hear it. It is a long story, a very long story and also a true life experience," said the old man.

"Yes, I would like to hear it," said Jane, "we like listening to long stories, especially true life stories."

"Okay," he said.

"One more thing, you have not told us your name," said Jane.

"Oh, yes," he replied, "sorry, my name is Tom. I live next door to you."

"Ah ha, no wonder you were coming to us very often before," Nora said.

"That is not the issue," said Jane, "what I do not understand is that he was drunk when we first met, yet he still remembers every single thing that happened."

"Oh yes, Jane, that is actually very strange because the way he was acting that day, it was as if he did not know what he was doing at all," Nora said.

"Were you pretending to be drunk, Tom? Please tell us," asked Jane.

Tom laughed and said: "I was only drunk, I was not insane, young ladies."

"Tom, you must be very intelligent," said Jane and Nora.

"Intelligent - it was not a matter of intelligence, but it had to do with saving my life," said Tom.

"You both saved me from myself because, if you had not called that young policeman, I would probably be history by now, because when that policeman left the scene, he followed me. When I was making my way to another restaurant he caught me while I was trying to cycle to the restaurant, without looking to the left or right, as a car was coming towards me. I took no notice but that young man drew me away, took the bike from me and took me home. He knows me and he is a very good young man. He lives about seven houses away from you and me, but I want you both to get this point - I never forgot your faces." Tom pointed at them.

"Still, we think you are very smart because we have forgotten almost everything that happened that day," said Jane and Nora.

"Oh, it is amazing the way things coincide," said Jane.

"Have you friends?" asked Nora.

"I have only one friend, and that is the young policeman you called," answered Tom.

"Alright Tom, we are going to be your friends too if you want," said Jane and Nora.

"Oh, great," said Tom.

"Tom, have you any family around here?" asked Nora.

Tom paused a little and said: "No, I live alone. My life is nothing to talk about, but as it is I'm going to tell you about me. Remember one of you asked me what happened to my left ear and I guess you still want to listen to the story in the book I'm holding. I am going to tell you everything," said Tom, "but, I repeat, it is a very long story."

"Tom, we are ready to listen to the a-z of that story; we are not in any kind of hurry, moreover, it is the weekend. Just give us two minutes and we will be back," said Jane and Nora.

They went into their house and returned with food and drinks which they gave to Tom, who had been feeling hungry but did not know how to tell them. Tom was delighted; he never expected such generosity and he looked at them in surprise. Jane and Nora noticed his expression and they immediately sat down beside Tom, tickled him and told him to stop guessing into an empty sky and eat his food and tell them the story before it got dark. Tom ate his food and did not say a word, but continued looking at them in a surprised manner. Jane took the book from Tom and started reading in a loud voice, while Nora was singing very loudly close to Tom's ear.

Tom shouted: "Oh, my ears - alright I'm going to tell you the story now."

"That's better!" Jane and Nora shouted in unison.

CHAPTER THREE

Tom tells his Life Story

"My real name is Thompson, Thompson Ogeechee. I am an old man, as you see and I want to start by telling you a bit about myself, before we go to the story in this book. I am sixty-eight years old and I used to be a soldier, but now I am retired and surviving on my pension and the rents. I own the house where I live and all the people you see in that house are my tenants. I sold the house you live in to the company you work for many years ago. I had some horrible experiences as a child. My mother died during childbirth. I had one brother and one sister and I'm the youngest. My father was a very hard-working man but, when things became very tough my father could not afford our school fees and, more importantly, my brother's fees, because he was in final year in university then studying to be a petroleum engineer. He went to one of our neighbours to borrow money but he would not give it to him, so my brother took the financial responsibility upon himself. He struggled because he was paying our school fees also.

"Suddenly my father fell ill and things became tougher than we anticipated. My brother was trying to finish his master's degree and at the same time he was trying to see that my sister and I continued with our education: plus he was trying to pay my father's hospital bills and for our food. My brother was earning a very good salary, but the family expenditure was far more than his income. He would go to work, come back late in the evening and go to the farm with me and my sister. Every weekend we spent most of our time at the farm. When my brother was transferred things became harder; my father's health was also deteriorating. My sister was very beautiful and many men came to ask her hand in marriage, but my brother kept turning them down, insisting that my sister must finish her education before she got married. Although we were very poor we had a very happy home; but that happiness went sour when my father gave my sister in marriage to a man we did not know very well, and still do not, even to this day.

"A few years later my father died. I was only seventeen when he died and my brother was twenty-five. The death of my father was very painful to us but what changed our life even more was that once my sister got married, we never saw her again. She did not come back, even when our father died. My brother loved us so much that he never allowed us to do any hard job, he never allowed me to go out and look for a job, even when I was on holiday from training to be a soldier, and never gave up the search for our sister. To cut a long story short, my brother later got details of the man who had married my sister. It turned out that he was a gangster, a fraud, an armed robber and worst of all was that he was polygamist. He had three wives already before my sister; and he was a cultist as well.

"A few years after my brother made this discovery, he died in a motor accident and I was left alone. I felt hopeless and had no interest in living. I returned to the search for my sister. I took all the details my brother left and went to my brother's grave and wept and promised my brother that I would find our sister. I did find my sister's husband but I never found my sister because I learned that she ran away from that bloody man many years earlier, so, out of anger and frustration, I shot Albert, my sister's husband, dead. That is why I am here today: I came to seek refuge in this country in order to run away from my criminal record. I married here and I had one son, Francis, whom I loved so much."

Tom went quiet and Jane asked him about Francis. He told them that Francis was dead.

"And your wife?" asked Nora.

"Oh, she left when Francis was ten years old," Tom answered.

"Why?" asked Jane.

"She was constantly complaining to me that I loved my sister and my brother more than her, because I used to tell my son about my sister and my brother all the time. She was always complaining that I was working too much and that if I got any chance, I discussed nothing but my sister and my brother. My son tried to make her understand that such things were not something one could forget easily, but she never listened. So she ran off with a man and all my weeping and pleadings could not stop her. Moreover, she did not take Francis into consideration before she made her decision.

"My son told me to forget her, that she did not care, not even for him, even though he was her only child. My son Francis was like a brother and a friend to me; he made me forget all my sorrows but suddenly my life became miserable again.

"It was one evening when my son came back from work, just at around 8pm, when I heard a knock on the door. I went and opened the door; it was three armed robbers. They were searching the house when my son came downstairs and one of the criminals saw him and yelled, 'Francis! Francis! Francis!' I went upstairs to get my gun. I was on the last step when Francis yelled, 'Father, Father, Oh my Father!' and then I saw my son lying in a pool of his own blood.

"I had no choice but to fight back. I shot two of the robbers dead but one of them escaped. I chased after him and shot him. I heard him scream but I ran back to check my son. Meanwhile, one of the remaining robbers, I mean the one that nearly escaped, shot me on my left ear, but I took no notice. Before I got back to the house our neighbours had taken my son to hospital. I collapsed and was rushed to the hospital and after several surgeries about five bullets were removed from my left ear. When I recovered, I was told that my son had died after fighting for his life. So that was how I lost my left ear.

"I'm surprised that you did not ask why I wear sunglasses all the time; I'm half blind as well. I cannot see very well with my left eye - so I'm not only a one-eared man, I am also a one eyed-old man. Many times I tried taking my own life but on each occasion I would hear my brother calling, 'Tom, Tom, Tom - do not do anything stupid', and in the nights I would hear a sound like a rushing wind. Within ten minutes, I would fall asleep and then I would be chatting and laughing with my son, Francis, just exactly the way we used to chat when he was alive. Before I knew what was happening it would be morning and each day before I woke up Francis would say, 'I have to go, father.' I would ask, 'Where?' I would wake up then and break down in tears.

"It was more than a dream because on many occasions my house could have been on fire, but mysteriously this was prevented by an unseen force. The first time, I was boiling water, forgot about it and the water dried up; there was smoke everywhere and I had fallen asleep while watching TV. I was dreaming about having a discussion with my brother."

"What were you discussing with him?" asked Nora.

"He was asking whether I had seen my sister."

"Oh," said Nora, "you did not tell us how the fire outbreak was prevented."

"While I was still talking to my brother, in my dream, he told me to go to the kitchen, calling me 'Tommie' as he used to when he was alive. When I reached the kitchen the kettle had already been taken from the cooker. On another occasion, I lit a candle to pray and after praying I slept on the couch. The papers I was reading caught fire while I was fast asleep. Suddenly I heard Francis, my son, say, 'Go upstairs, Dad, and be careful.' I woke to see that the curtains were almost burnt down. What stopped the fire still remains a mystery to me."

Jane and Nora suggested that Tom's brother and his son were his guardian angels. Tom said that they were not far from the truth.

"Tom, would it not have been better if you remarried after the death of your son? At least you were not old then, according to your story," said Jane. "Or did you not think of that after all you have been through, Tom?"

"Well, I never thought of it, even though many people suggested it to me, but I couldn't convince myself to get married again because of the reason why my wife had left. I did not want any woman to come into my house and leave again for the same reason. I love my brother and I love my son - my son meant the whole world to me. I get comfort and companionship from my son and my brother every passing moment of my life. That young policeman is like a son to me; I feel complete, the same way I used to feel when my Francis was alive.

"When that policeman is not around, when I sit down, I tell my brother to sit at my left hand side and Francis to sit by my right. I do this because I believe they are still very much around me, even though they are dead. Most times, once I sit down, I snooze and chat with my son and brother. Once the young policeman comes, they tell me they have to leave me with a better company, and then I wake up immediately. He sleeps at my house sometimes if he feels I do not look well or happy.

"I was hospitalized three times: first for post-traumatic stress disorder and then with high blood pressure. I remember being in a coma one time, when I found myself in a very beautiful environment. I was very happy but, all of a sudden, my brother and my son told me to go and complete my mission. When I woke up I saw the policeman sitting by my side. I did not know how I got to the hospital so he told me."

Jane and Nora were both in tears but they did not want Tom to notice while he continued his story. Suddenly he could see that the two girls were disturbed by his story; he felt sorry and stopped talking. Nora asked him, if he had found out why the robbers had killed his son. Tom kept quiet, but Jane and Nora tickled him and Tom laughed and told them they should forget about the story and think of other things. Jane and Nora insisted he should answer their question. Tom told them they should forget all the things from the past and press forward.

"Tears might flow like a river but out of the same tears comes joy. The world itself is full of tears and joy; women go through tears and after the tears comes the joy of motherhood, so, Tom, answer this last question," said Jane.

Tom cleared his throat saying: "Well said, your words are full of wisdom. I will answer your question. After all, if there is no death, there would be no life either. Death is the inevitable destiny of man; it is a debt we all are going to pay. To answer your question, yes, I know why the robbers killed my son. The boy that killed him went to the same university as my son, so he was afraid that Francis would reveal his identity to the police, and that was why he killed him. The guy that I shot, the one that ran away, told the police when they found him in the bush."

"What happened to him after?" asked the two girls.

"I learned that he did not live to face any form of justice; he died two days after he was brought to the hospital by the police," said Tom.

"Girls, I think we have spent a long time here, it is getting dark and we have to go inside," he said.

As soon as Tom finished talking Nora said she could hear a voice calling, 'Dad'.

They all kept quiet and the voice called again and Tom said: "That is my son, the policeman, calling me. I must be on my way into the house. Anyway, young ladies, that is my story and also the content of the book. I am the author of the book and the rest you can read by yourselves. Here, take."

Tom gave the book to the two girls. When he turned to go Jane and Nora held him by the hand and said: "We will go with you."

So they went with Tom to his house where they met the young policeman. The two girls spent an hour with Tom and the young police.

CHAPTER FOUR

Tom Falls Ill Again

Jane and Nora left Tom and the policeman and went to their own house. That night they agreed with each other that they were going to look for Tom's sister. If she was alive, they decided that they would go and see her and bring her to Tom, and if she was dead, they would bring Tom to her grave. Jane and Nora decided to be responsible for making Tom's food. The young policeman had little or no time because he had to go from work to college every evening. Also, unknown to Tom, he never gave up the search for Tom's sister.

The next day Jane and Nora came back from work and went to Tom's house to say hello, but Tom was not there. They were worried because they thought he had gone drinking. While they were still wondering they heard a sudden sound. Jane said it sounded very familiar. "Yes, you are right, it is not anything new. I guess Tom has started his hide and seek games again," said Nora.

"Tom, Tom, Tom - come out from wherever you are, your dinner is ready," yelled Nora. There was no sign of Tom who was hiding behind the curtain. While Jane and Nora went upstairs to check whether he was there, he ran out and went to the kitchen and started eating the food they had brought him. Jane and Nora then went outside to ask the neighbours whether they had seen Tom. When they came back they saw Tom, who was now lying down on the sofa watching TV.

"Which way did you go, Tom?" they asked.

"I did not go anywhere, I was inside the house, right behind you, but you were so busy thinking that I had gone drinking that you did not bother to trace the sound you heard."

The girls still had their doubts about where Tom had been so he told them to go into the kitchen where they would see a sign and stop doubting him. They went to the kitchen and saw that

Tom had finished his food. While they were on their way to the kitchen, Tom looked after them and wondered whether they were really humans or angels. The girls came back from the kitchen and sat down. Tom laughed and told them not to worry about him, that he neither drank nor smoked.

"Young ladies, you worry so much. I started drinking because I was lonesome and it became a habit until that young man came into my life and saved me from myself," said Tom.

"It's okay, Tom, you are a very wise man and we love you the way you are even when you are drunk," said Jane and Nora.

"Yes, I love him the way he is too. Tom is a very handsome man - I wonder how he was when he was young," said the young policeman who had just arrived. He went in and ate his food which has been prepared by Jane and Nora.

The girls sat down with the policeman to listen to the stories Tom told them every night. After the stories Tom told Jane and Nora that the policeman had a name and that they should stop calling him 'police guy'.

"His name is Larry," said Tom.

"My name is Jane," said Jane.

"Call me Nora, that's my name," said Nora also.

"You all know who I am, but I do not know you - I mean Jane and Nora," said Tom.

Nora told Tom and Larry every detail about herself and Larry did likewise. By then Tom's eyes were heavy so Larry said they should go to bed and continue from where they stopped the next evening; so they broke up.

Larry went up to Tom's bedroom and met Tom as he was coming out from the bathroom.

"Hello boy," said Tom.

"Oh, hi Dad, I thought you were already asleep."

"No son, it's pretty early but I don't know why I was falling asleep in that sofa; probably I ate too much," said Tom.

"Might be," said Larry. "Dad, those two ladies are very nice, thank God we met them and thank God also that you went to comfort yourself with alcohol that day, otherwise we wouldn't know these pretty ladies. Moreover, I now know that I do not know how to cook, so at least we are eating good food. I hope they won't go on transfer."

"Yes, they are good. I have never seen such nice young ladies, but as for the pretty aspect of them, I don't know. You know I am old but I know that they both are very tall, and one is taller, she is almost as tall as me."

"Oh yes, that's Jane," said Larry.

"I did not know; I get mixed up with their names but I think one is quieter than the other, but they are very nice and kind," said Tom.

Larry discussed Jane frequently, always taking his time to describe her to Tom. He was very fond of Jane, to the extent that once he got back home from work the first question would be, where is Jane? Tom noticed too that Larry constantly wanted to sit close to Jane.

"Ah ha, that reminds me, Dad, did you look at Jane very well?" Larry asked.

"No," said Tom, "what about her?"

"She looks very like you - even her long legs, and her face is exactly like your son's face, the way she talks, her looks and her movement. Take a good look when next they come around. I wonder whether she is, by any chance, your sister's daughter?" asked Larry.

Tom laughed and said it was not possible.

"Larry," Tom called, "I am beginning to see that you have special interest in that Jane, because I do hear you telling her to be careful always, even when she wants to sit down. You definitely want something from her, which I do not know. But anyway, one day we will find out." He then added: "I think I have to sleep now."

"Okay," said Larry.

As he hugged Tom he noticed that he was very warm and he asked him if he was feeling alright.

"I think I'm getting cold and fever," answered Tom.

"Then I have to sleep with you," said Larry, "but first let me inform the girls. Remember, I'm going away tomorrow for four days."

The next morning Larry took Tom to the hospital as he had been very sick during the night. After three days Tom was discharged home and Nora and Jane looked after him. Nora had arranged to visit her parents and would not be back for two weeks, while Larry was to come back on Saturday. On Saturday night Larry, Tom and Jane were discussing Tom's illness. Larry had always wanted to know Jane's historical background, but had never had a chance to discuss with her privately, because Jane is a very shy type of person. So Larry, seeing an opportunity to get closer to Jane, asked her to tell them who she was.

"We have heard from your friend Nora and I think it's time you tell us who you are," said Larry.

"Oh me, I have no origin - forget it. I am independent, just an autonomous individual," Jane said.

"I do not believe in individual autonomy because you belong to a family, a community, and society at large," argued Larry.

"Where do you come from originally? At least let us start from there," said Larry.

"I come from the middle of nowhere, I told you that before, and I have no identity," said Jane.

"Please answer my question, Jane, don't evade it," Larry said with curiosity.

"Why not ask Nora about me, because she knows everything? Anyhow, it would be better if we discussed arrangements regarding who is going to look after Tom while we are at work, instead of this non-issue about me," Jane continued.

"Oh, yes, you are right. It is an urgent issue. We have to bring someone to stay with him from the time we go to work till we come back," Larry suggested.

"That is a good idea and I will be responsible for the payment while you look for a nice fellow to look after Tom, because you know many more people than I do," Jane said.

"I do not think Tom will have a problem with payment. I am pretty sure that he has more than enough," Larry responded.

"Yes, I know and I can see that myself," said Jane, "but do not discuss anything about that with him. I just want him to be comfortable - he needs spiritual and emotional freedom because he has been through a lot. He needs liberation from the cage of loneliness and we have to liberate him. We are like grandchildren to him, and he is seventy now so we have to do our best for him," Jane suggested.

"Yes," said Larry, "but what of your friend? Do you think it is going to be okay with her?"

"Oh, yes. If I say no, Nora will say no and if I say yes, she will also say yes. Where she stands, I stand there too, so that is not a problem," answered Jane.

"Alright then, we have a deal," Larry said happily.

Tom was fast asleep while all the arguments and plans were going on. Jane stood up to go and Larry asked her if she would answer one question.

Jane said, "Yes, I can answer as many questions as you like to ask, thank God, it is the weekend."

"Are you related to Tom by any chance?" asked Larry.

"No, not in any way. I did not know him before; I do not know who he is but I like him," Jane replied.

"Do you know you look like Tom?" asked Larry.

"Well, I do not know, but you are the seventh person to tell me that I look like Tom, but I think it is just because my skin is light and his skin is light too. Moreover, I am very tall and he is very tall as well. But people say that my movement is like his although I do not believe it - do you think it is true?" asked Jane.

"Yes," said Larry, "and the second question I wanted to ask you …"

"Please can I go?" Jane pleaded.

Larry held Jane by the hand saying: "I am sorry."

"Sorry for what?"

"I am just sorry; but can you spend a night with me and Tom, because you and I have a lot to discuss?" Larry beckoned.

"I am not sure, I have to go; whatever it is should wait till tomorrow; so can I go?" Jane anxiously asked again.

"Fine," Larry said and, following Jane to their door step, he caught her by the hand and kissed her.

Jane shouted in a surprised manner: "What did you do that for?"

"How I wish I knew," said Larry, still holding Jane's hand, but when he saw that Jane was angry, he quickly left and said: "Okay, good night, we can continue tomorrow."

Larry stood at the door until Jane locked it and he shouted out loud: "Be careful beautiful."

"Alright then, good night," said Jane.

Larry left and very early in the morning, before Tom woke up, Larry had gone to collect Jane.

One week later Nora came back and Larry got a job as an accountant in a bank and was posted to the eastern part of Nigeria. When Larry left, Jane and Nora moved into Tom's house as Larry advised. Tom was very happy with his home help and Jane and Nora tried to maintain the home help as long as they could. Meanwhile Larry was ringing the house all the time, mostly to talk to Jane.

CHAPTER FIVE

Jane Reveals her Identity

One night Jane and Nora said to Tom: "Larry told us a lot about himself, but we never heard him say anything about his parents."

"Larry ran away from home at the age of fourteen because his father had a drink problem and his mother remarried. Two years later his father died in a car accident. He went to his mother but his mother rejected him so he was lonely. He met another lonely man, who is now his father; he is a promising young man," said Tom.

"It is amazing that a mother can reject her child. I wonder how they manage. One might ask how they sleep and wake up without that child; eat, drink and get around their daily activities without that child. If that child is dead, at least you know where he or she is, but if that child is alive and you as a mother do not care about his or her safety, the shelter, provision or protection of that child, it is horrible," said Jane.

'I think it takes a horrible heart to do horrible things," Nora suggested.

"Yes, I think so too, but not only that. Some women are very materialistic, because, in the case of Larry, the man his mother met was very wealthy, and she thought the world was a bed of roses, but she did not know that we are not self-made, that there is a great force behind our existence, and not only that, she forgot that there is accountability, so I think it takes a combination of a horrible heart, as Nora said, and materialism for a woman to reject her child," Tom explained.

'Oh yes, Tom, you have a strong point there," said Jane. "I have now seen reasons why someone can reject her child but I don't understand the reason why a mother will choose to abandon an innocent baby in a dump. That raises a constant question in my heart and the question still remains - what is a family? As far as I know, no one has satisfied me with an answer to that question. When I was at university in Lagos, a boy in my department said a family involves a wider network that includes parents, brothers and sisters, uncles, aunts and grandparents, while others say that a family is a social construction, consisting of parents and their offspring. During our youth service, Nora, remember we interviewed some of those boys that live on the streets of Lagos and Abuja, and they had a different view of a family? They said that your family is made up of the people around you, the ones that are happy with you, and are willing to accept you; that it does not mean that your family is your parents and your siblings, because your parents may not be there for you in times of trouble, but your friends may be; so I think it is people that care for you that make up your family. Nora, remember, that was what one of the street boys said?"

Nora nodded her head. Jane continued talking, describing what one of those street boys said: "One of those boys explained that he was the only child of his parents, but that they didn't care for him, so he decided to make it on his own. He pointed out his friend, Charles, and explained to me that they did everything together. 'He cares for me so he is my family,' that boy said. I agree with what that boy said and believe that if we had interviewed them further, we would have discovered that they had a wide emotional landscape," said Jane.

"I have parents and sister and brothers," said Nora, "but here I am very happy and content and, despite the wealth of my parents, I live here and visit my family. This is not because they hate me or anything, but because I'm grown up and I know what I want and where I want to be. My parents love me very much; my sister and my brothers even cry whenever I leave home. But I like Jane and you, Tom, and right now you are my family, but when I go to my parents' home, they are my family too."

"The two of you are very wise and the most intelligent ladies I have ever met in my entire life. I always feel that there might be a connection between the three of you - I mean you Jane, Nora and Larry, because Larry is as reasonable as the two of you," said Tom. "Coming back to what we were discussing, I think both of you are right with your findings and philosophy because if we take it back to the Jesus movement, you can recall vividly that when his mother and father were looking for him, they found him in the midst of a multitude. When his mother told him that they had been looking for him, he told them that the people he was with were his mother and father. That does not mean that he hated his parents, but at that particular moment, that was where he found comfort, friendship, companionship and joy, so the idea of a family has a wide range of understanding and definitions.

"I was almost a dead man who was in love with my job. I can remember when I was a little boy, whenever my father asked me what I wanted to become when I grew up, the answer was always 'army officer', and that dream came true. I lost my brother and my sister, my wife left and my son died. I became hopeless and my job became my family. Then, suddenly, I became a slave to the bottle which was also my family. Then I met Larry who saved me from the bondage of self-destruction; he lifted me up in some ways and I lifted him up in some ways, and together we became father and child. He is now my family; he means everything to me. Just look at the two of you and think of how we met, and here we are today. Things are not always what they seem, and one thing that terrifies me about this world is the way it spins around; yet it is unimaginably deep and we are going far, farther than we can imagine.

"Now, however, I think it is time for us to start work. Remember you said we are cleaning the house inside out today and Larry is coming back the day after tomorrow," said Tom.

"Oh no, Tom, you are going to sit on the high stool while we do the cleaning. All you need do is put on your glasses to look like an old philosopher. Your work is to just observe and criticize because you have not recovered fully from your illness," said Nora.

Tom wore his glasses and his hat and sat on the high stool while Jane and Nora cleaned and changed the position of everything in the house. When they finished cleaning Jane asked Tom about Larry's mother and whether Larry later reconciled with her.

"Well, I think it is better to forgive than to seek revenge because forgiveness is a window to a great lesson, and a doorway to comfort, relationship and friendship. I stained my hands with blood in the past in the name of revenge, and I have come to realize that I am not an embodiment of goodness. There are two sides to a coin and so too with humans. We all have two sides - the good side and the bad side - even a criminal has his good side and bad side. I also know that if one door does not close that the other one cannot open," said Tom.

"Remember David, the shepherd boy? He said that he passed through the valley of the shadow of death and goodness and mercy followed him, so also I think we have to pass through the valley of the shadow of death before we can say goodness and mercy shall follow us. But I want you to get one thing right, and that is no matter how long we live, life is just so short. Coming back to Larry, I have told you a bit, the rest you will hear from him," Tom concluded.

"Oh Tom, you are full of knowledge and understanding, and from your life we have learned that time heals the wound but one must not allow that time to slip away from our hands. Moreover, if we let go of some things and accept who we are, the world will be a better and simpler place to live in. We have learned a lot in few minutes, and I think Tom's words are very inspirational and very confrontational to those of us, who think they are nothing," said Nora.

"Jane, I borrowed this statement from you," Nora continued, "because sometimes we think or say we have no origin because we have not looked at both sides." Nora went further saying: "I think when we discuss our problem with our loved ones we dance a new dance and sing a new song."

Tom clapped and said with a laugh: "Well said, young lady well said."

Jane was so cold she did not talk. Tom kept wondering what could have made her so cold, but he wanted Nora to find out. Nora asked Jane if there was anything she wanted to discuss with Tom. Jane said 'No' and warned Nora to leave her alone.

"Oh, I forgot to tell you, superfluity and self-preoccupation come sooner than white hairs, while competency and simplicity live longer, am I right?" Nora asked.

"Oh yes, pretty well," Tom replied.

"Ah ha, one more thing, I was crying that I have no shoes until I saw someone who has no legs. Do you like my statement, Tom?" asked Nora.

"Oh sure, very much. It is full of meaning," said Tom.

Jane stood up in anger and said that some people have never been through pain and that some people are also born with silver spoons in their mouths and despite that, they talk anyhow. Tom responded: "If I was born with a silver spoon in my mouth, I would have been worse than an idiot, and might be that if my brother did not die. I would have been worse than a dummy because he loved me so much and he never liked me doing anything in the house; but we have to respect the disparity of destiny."

Nora asked Jane to sit down and she sat beside her. Nora asked her if she had something to discuss but Jane stated angrily that she did not have anything to discuss and called Nora a parrot. Nora reminded Jane of the time she previously had recited a poem for her and that it was her turn to recite one.

"Oh, Mother Teresa or the Pope - which one are you? Please spare me the gospel and let me have your so-called poem quickly," said Jane with anger.

"Well," said Nora, "I'm going to be brief. The poem goes like this," and she recited it:

The loss of gold is much
The loss of honour is more
The loss of time, such a loss
As no man can restore.

"You cannot restore the loss of time simply because you cannot delay or fast forward nature," explained Nora.

Jane pushed Nora angrily and went upstairs. Nora broke down in tears and told Tom of the time when Jane told her own poem, and Nora did not push her. Tom called Jane back and spoke to the two of them and afterwards Jane went upstairs. Then Tom asked Nora why Jane had become so upset and Nora answered that it was because she had asked Jane if she wanted to discuss it.

"Discuss what?" Tom asked.

"The answer lies with her," answered Nora.

"In that case you have to go up to her," Tom suggested.

"No, she is going to push me away, I know her more than you do," Nora replied.

"She may not. You never know until you try," Tom said. "Wait a minute, don't worry, I will come up to the room after you. She won't do any such thing while I'm there."

Nora went to the kitchen, prepared tea in a jug and took it upstairs. Just then the phone rang. It was Larry who said he was at the door. So Tom quickly opened the door and Nora ran out to welcome him. But Jane did not come down and Larry was wondering where she was. Tom said they should all go upstairs.

When Jane saw Larry she smiled and said welcome.

Tom said: "It is good to see a smile on your face again."

"Did anything happen?" asked Larry.

"Oh no, nothing happened, it is just that sometimes we find it difficult to forget the past and face present and the future, and I think the best way to go about it is to discuss the past, push it aside and press forward," said Nora.

"Yes," said Larry, "I have a long story behind me, friends, and I'm going to tell you because Tom here made me what I am today."

"I already told them a bit, son," said Tom.

"I used to be a policeman before I met Tom. You all know I never liked it, but Tom gave me a new life and a new hope. He paid my school fees. I was living in the barracks and he gave me an apartment in one of his houses. He brought me into his home and got me out of police business and, most importantly, he made me see and forgive my mother," said Larry.

"How do you mean 'forgive' and where is your mother?" asked Jane.

"Well, she died, but before her death I swore never to have anything to do with her, until Tom made me see the importance of forgiveness. I had raised a curse on her many times; I had gone to her and she rejected me. One day she came to see me while I was with my friends and she warned me not to come to her house again. I was pleading with her and crying but she never looked back. The next day I went to her house to plead; again she rejected me and her husband pushed me away. Then I lifted up my voice in a tone of grief and agony, saying to her,

'This family will know no peace until I find comfort.' Years later, Tom told me that I had found comfort in my life and that it was time for me to forgive my mother, so I forgave her. A few years later she died, and this is my story," said Larry.

"Oh, great," said Nora, "so do you want to discuss it now, Jane?" she pleaded.

"Yes, I think you are right. It is time for me to let that cat out of the bag," said Jane.

"I was born to die, my mother threw me away in the dump and a woman picked me up. I thought this woman was my mother, but when she was dying in the hospital she told me that she was not my biological mother. She explained that she knew my mother, but she did not know who my father was. I had been asking her who my father was, so, as she was sick and knew she was going to die, she felt it was time to tell me who I am," Jane said.

"Where did this happen and when did it happen?" asked Tom.

"It happened twenty-three years ago in this city of Lagos," answered Jane.

"Where in particular in the city of Lagos did it happen?" asked Tom.

"Well, it happened in Ikeja cantonment. When a senior army officer came to the cantonment she fell in love with him and tried to force the man to marry her. The man explained to her that it was not so long since he had lost his son and that he needed time to come out of himself; that he wanted his wound to heal naturally and that he did not want to rush. But because she, my mother, was very hasty, pompous and predominant, according to my mother - I mean the woman I thought was my mother - she did not listen. I learned that her parents were very rich and that they used to despise people a lot, which was the reason she did not live with her first husband. Did I answer your question, Tom?" asked Jane.

'Yes," said Tom, "but did that woman tell you the name of that lady, the name of the army officer and what the lady was doing when she was alive? Did she tell you how long that army officer stayed?" asked Tom.

"She did not tell me her name because I did not ask, but she did tell me that my biological mother told her that if she picked me, that she should name me Jane. This was because the senior army officer had told her that if ever he was to have a child again, and if she was a girl, that he would name her Jane, and that if he was a boy that he would call him Francis. She said that the baby had a birthmark in exactly the same position as the army officer and that it was same type of birthmark. She also said that the woman told her that the army officer stayed for six months and that my biological mother was a solicitor," Jane explained.

"How did the woman you thought was your mother know that your biological mother was going to throw her baby away?" asked Larry.

"Oh, that lady that brought me up, my mother - I call her mother even now because she is my mother as far as I am concerned - was a midwife who had no child of her own, and my biological mother delivered me in the hospital where she was working. According to her, she was monitoring her closely, because she suspected that my biological mother was not going to keep the baby. She said my biological mother had come to the hospital twice to abort the baby, but they prevented her. Finally, one of the doctors promised her that he was going to take the baby from her when it was born but, unfortunately, the doctor went on transfer. When she learned that the doctor was gone on transfer her countenance changed so, when she was discharged, the midwife followed my mother and continued following after her until she got to the dump. I thought that the midwife was too old to be my mother, but whenever I told Nora she would say that I worried too much. Whatever may be the case, this is me, here," Jane said.

"Jane, you said something about a birthmark - can I see the birthmark, please?" pleaded Tom.

"Yes, it's here," Nora quickly rolled up Jane's sleeve and the birthmark was right below her shoulder on her right hand side, exactly where Tom had his one.

Tom was shocked when he saw the birthmark, but he managed to say: "Jane, soon your story will become my story."

"Did your mother throw you away, Tom?" Jane asked.

"My mother did not throw me away," answered Tom.

"Then what happened?" asked Larry.

Tom was lost in the world of his own; he was motionless. They kept wondering what had sent him into his shell. He asked them to give him a minute and he went downstairs and wept. When he came back to them he sat down beside Jane and said: "I made a mistake, I made a mistake. I would have gone to see her only she was too pompous and arrogant for my liking. I don't like people that attach so much importance to material things. I went to her and she treated me like a piece of rubbish because I did not allow her to impose her opinion on me."

They thought Tom was going insane; Larry was so worried that he suggested they take Tom to a psychiatric hospital, but Tom told them not to panic, that nothing was wrong with him.

"If nothing is wrong with you, Tom, why the sudden change in your behaviour?" asked Nora.

"It is nothing much, it is just that I know the lady, I mean Jane's biological mother, and her biological father - he is still alive," Tom answered.

"If you know where he is, tell us, Tom, tell us. I want to look for him. I will do anything to make Jane happy, even if it warrants spilling the last drop of my blood; I am ready to do that," Larry confessed.

"You want to look for him, but does Jane want to look for him?" Tom asked.

"Oh yes, with all my heart. You do not know what I go through all the time - I'm a prisoner of my emotions because everybody has someone to talk about but who do I talk about? The woman who saved me from death is no more. If it were not for my friend Nora, and she is not just my friend, she is my sister ..." Jane said tearfully.

Nora moved close to Jane saying: "Weep not, the worst of it is over. You were born to live, you were not born to die, and it was like that so that you would not only have a history, but that you would be stronger, wiser and more sympathetic to help those in similar circumstances."

Tom clapped for Nora and then removed his shirt. They were all shocked to see the same birthmark as Jane had on Tom's arm. Tom said: "I am the army officer. I did not know your mother was pregnant before I left, but from the very first time I met her, she was pushing for marriage. I did tell her I was not interested, but that if I ever had a child again, that I would give him my son's name if he was a boy and if she was a girl, that I would call her Jane, my sister's name. You see this birthmark? It is in my family; we got it from my father, my brother had it, my sister has it, I have it and my son had it also, all in the same position and now my daughter, Jane, has it as well."

Jane was taken aback, but Larry, who had always been telling Tom and Nora that Jane was very like Tom, was not surprised at all. There was a lot of happiness and tears of joy at the end of the long night.

"I had a happy family but death tore my life apart. Then, today, my eyes have seen the unbelievable. Although it was like a dream and a tale in the beginning, now it is real. My tears of yesteryear are wiped forever, because my name will not be forgotten when I'm gone. If I close my eyes in death tomorrow, it is all well, because my heart is full of joy and my spirit is filled with gladness," said Tom.

Two days later Nora and Larry organized a party for Tom and Jane and invited some friends and neighbours. It was a very happy occasion and, as usual, Larry, Jane and Nora went to Tom's room to listen to his stories before they went to bed. This time Nora broke down in tears, leaving the others wondering what had happened. Jane persuaded Nora to talk to them.

"It might be the wrong time to say this, but I think it is the best time to say it - I thank everybody very much, especially my dear friend, Jane. I think it is time to say farewell to everybody because I want to go back to stay with my family. This does not mean that I am going to stay away forever. I will still come as often as I can," said Nora.

The next day Nora went to her parents with Jane and after one week Jane went back to Larry and her father, Tom. While Jane was away Larry told Tom that he wanted to marry Jane. Tom smiled, "I knew it would come to this; when you were away, you spoke to Jane on the phone for seven hours; Jane and Nora told me. I presume you have told her?" Tom enquired.

"Not really, she is too shy and too quiet. Jane talks sparingly so I want to follow her the way she is, to avoid mistake, because I do not want to be too fast, thereby making her angry. Jane is very sensitive," Larry explained.

"I understand but you have to talk to her first, because I cannot decide for her. As for the sensitivity it is in our family. I have taken a good look at Jane she is really my daughter. I see a lot of my mother in her," Tom confessed.

"I love Jane. I have been hiding my feelings for her for a very long time, but I think it is time to show it. Since she left," Larry continued, "I have not been myself. I cannot wait to set my eyes on her next week. She is a paragon."

"I do not know about her beauty, but you must hear this, you are my son and Jane is my daughter. Always treat Jane like your junior sister, whether I am alive or dead. Settle your disputes behind closed doors. Do not give a chance to the meticulous interlopers," Tom advised.

"Thanks Tom," Larry said. "I am scared of proposing to Jane because I cannot handle it if she says no," he confessed.

"Jane is only a human. You just have to pick up courage and talk to her, the worst she could say is no. Moreover I do not think she is going to say no. After all, is she not the same person you conversed on the phone with, for several hours every day when you were away?" Tom asked.

"Yes she is," Larry replied.

"Then, I do not see the possibility of a 'no' answer," Tom maintained.

CHAPTER SIX

The Echo of a Troubled Soul

When Nora got home her parents handed in a note to her. The note was written by one of her old school friends. Nora's mother explained to her that they were glad that she had come home, because they were about to send for her.

"Why?" Nora curiously asked.

"Because that young man was constantly disturbing us here. I am sure he thought we did not want him to see you, which was why I made him write a note. Moreover you know it is difficult to get you on the phone, because most times you could not be bothered to answer your calls. Also I was not sure if you want me to give him your number," Nora's mother explained.

"What is his name? What does he want? Where does he come from?" Nora anxiously asked.

"Sorry I did not ask," Nora's mother stammered.

"Mom can you describe him?" Nora asked.

"How I wish I could. No more questions, read the note while I take my leave," Nora's mother ordered and left.

While Nora was trying to read the letter, the doorbell rang. It was the young man who wrote the letter. His name is John. John was the boy who stole Jane's notebook when they were in the university.

Nora was surprised to see John. She asked: "What brought you here? What do you want? Did you bring Jane's notebook? How come you told my parents that you are my old school friend?" Nora was trying to ask another question but John pleaded to come in first. Nora allowed him in.

"Can you answer my questions now that you are sitting down?" Nora urged.

"I am going to answer your questions, but I do not know where to start because you asked too many questions," John explained.

"John you heard me, you can start anywhere, all I know is that I need answers please," Nora appealed.

"Alright I just took that notebook because I did not know how to approach you and your friend. I always wanted to talk to you but you and your friend were the most difficult girls to approach in that campus. What do you expect from a desperate young man who was trying to express his feelings to a young lady he loves very much? Even the notebook did not solve my problem. I thought the two of you would have come to ask for the notebook, but you never bothered."

"Well that is by the way. I am here now; I have been searching for you for many years. At last I found you and I hope you will understand this time," John requested.

"Understand what?" Nora asked.

"Understand that I love you, I made every effort to get closer to you during our school days but you and your friend were so reserved that guys were afraid of talking to you. You are very responsible intelligent young ladies. I know. I was a torn in your flesh but I did not know what I was doing. I wanted positive attention from you but I did not get it; so I tried the negative ways of getting the attention I needed, but that did not work either; so I am just saying I am sorry," John apologized.

"Well lover boy, I have heard you but this is not the time to discuss love. And by the way what is written inside this paper?" Nora stretched out her hand and gave John the note. "I wanted to read it but now you are here tell me what you wrote." Nora compelled John to read the note.

John laughed and took the note from Nora saying, "that will not be necessary; I have already told you." He tore up the note.

After a few months of friendship John proposed marriage to Nora, who reciprocated by saying yes. Larry in like manner had proposed to Jane as well. Like Nora, Jane accepted the proposal. It was an entirely new life for Jane. A few years later she got married to Larry and they had two children. Nora also got married to John and had two children but she continued visiting Jane.

Some years later Nora lost her mother. Once, when Nora's father was in the hospital, Nora took her children to Jane's house, so that she would be free to look after her father and her husband could continue his work. One evening when Nora went to visit her father in the hospital he told her that he was being discharged the next day. Nora was very happy so she rang Jane and told her the news and said that she would call over the next day to collect her children. Little did she know that it would be a number of days before she could get to Jane's house?

While driving away from the hospital she saw a little boy sitting by the roadside crying. She stopped to ask him what was wrong but the little boy did not reply. So Nora got out of her car to talk to him. A man appeared from nowhere and ordered her at gunpoint to get into her car. As she got in she saw a man sitting in the driver's seat and another in the front passenger side. She tried to shout but they ordered her to shut up or she would be dead; so she sat in the back with the third man. A short distance later the man pushed her out of the car and they drove off in a direction she did not know.

Nora was helpless; she did not know where she was and she had no phone to make contact with anyone. She found herself in a dilemma, sitting by the roadside crying and it was getting very dark. Meanwhile, Jane and Larry were getting worried because it was long past the time she told them she would come to the house. Larry suggested they ring her husband in case she had gone home, but Jane insisted that she knew Nora very well and that she would have rung her if she were at home. When Nora's husband rang Larry told him that Nora and Jane had gone for a walk, while the children were in bed. Nora's children did not suspect anything.

It was getting very late. A man stopped to help Nora but she would not accept his offer of a lift. He told her that the sooner she left that area the better it would be for her, but Nora was adamant. The man left her and drove on a little, looked through his side mirror and saw Nora still sitting there. He went back and said to her: "If you love yourself, you'd better reason properly before darkness covers you. I'm taking my leave but I just pity your condition. I live not too far away from here, but I just want you to know that this place is a danger zone. Sit down here and continue to cry like a big baby if that is what you want, but I'm on my way to my house."

He left and Nora stood up and started running; she ran such a long way that she could barely speak from exhaustion. As she was staggering she saw a woman and three children sitting in front of a house, a big house, and she ran to them and fell down in front of them. The woman asked who she was but all she managed to say was 'water' three times. The woman gave her water and took her inside where she gave her food and a room to sleep in. The woman did not tell her husband and warned her children not to tell him either.

Around 11 pm the woman of the house went to the bedroom to talk to her husband when her children had gone to bed. Her husband was half asleep as she said to him: "Chris, a stranger works as if he is homeless. Man is the architect of his own problem. I believe that if we can help each other things will be much easier, because we don't know who is going to be there for us in the time of trouble. It might be a total stranger."

"You are right," her husband answered.

"Sometimes strangers are angels, I mean angels of light, and they can be angels of destruction too, but I believe that a mountain we cannot climb will never stand before us," continued the woman.

"You are right again, but why are you speaking in parables?" asked the husband.

"Well, heaven's light forever shine, earth's shadows fly, but wherever the pendulum swings …" She did not complete the statement.

Her husband stood in anger, saying: "Please spare me the lamentation, I have had enough of it. Talk and let me go to bed."

"Okay, I do not know how to say it or how you will feel about it. The most difficult part of it is that I don't know where to start," said the wife.

"Maybe you can start from the middle, so that I can go to bed," her husband replied.

"Okay, we have a visitor," said the wife.

"You didn't tell me you were expecting anybody," the husband replied.

The wife said she was not expecting anybody, nor did she even know the visitor herself, but that she accepted her because she did not know who would be there for her on the day of her death. There was a very strong argument between the two of them but at the end of it, her husband said he would like to meet the visitor. She took him to their guestroom, he saw Nora and shouted: "You again! How did you get here?"

Nora said she was sorry.

"Do you know her?" his wife asked.

"I met this lady many miles away from here, crying helplessly, and I tried to help her but she refused to talk to me. I went to her three times but she did not say a word and now she is here, in my house. Who are you?" the man asked Nora.

Nora introduced herself and told them her story. They were compassionate and kind to her and allowed her to use their phone, so Nora rang Jane and told her she would come back the next day and that they should try and take her father home from the hospital the next morning. Jane tried to question Nora, to find out where she was and why she was not going home, but Nora told Jane that she was in a place she did not know herself, that she should not worry and that she would tell her all about it the next day.

When Nora finished talking to Jane, the man and the woman introduced themselves to her. The man said: "Call me Chris - my wife might have told you, I'm Chris Ogeechee." Then, as he turned his back to go, Nora spotted a birthmark similar to that of Tom and Jane. Nora quickly recollected that Tom told them that his sister and brother also had this same birthmark.

Nora said to the man: "Oh my goodness, you are very tall."

Chris was very tall but Nora said it to delay him so that she could take a good look at the birthmark.

"Yes he is," the wife said, "and our three kids are very tall too. Don't take any notice of him because he is always in a hurry and he is running away now because he does not want to talk with us again."

Chris laughed, saying: "My mother was very tall and she told me that her father was also very tall, and so are her two brothers. Good night ladies," he said and left.

"He has a birthmark exactly like his mother," said Chris's wife.

Nora and the wife talked for a long time. Nora understood from their discussion that Chris's mother had died a few weeks earlier and that they had three children, whose names were

Henry, Thomas (who they called Tommie) and Jane. She also learned that Christopher was the name of Chris' grandfather, Henry was named after his mother's older brother, while Tommie was named after his mother's youngest brother, and Jane was named after his mother.

Nora felt a mounting of anxiety but she continued seeking answers. She asked her about Chris' father, who she discovered was dead. Nora asked her whether he had died of old age or illness.

"He was killed," Chris' wife replied.

"How, or rather why was he killed, if you don't mind me asking you?" Nora asked anxiously.

Chris' wife hissed shook her head and told Nora that it was a very long story which she was not ready to tell her, because it was a secret between herself and her husband. Nora asked her whether she knew Chris' father or whether she had met him. She answered: "Not even my husband knows his father, he does not know what he look like."

Nora continued pestering her but the woman eventually stood up and insisted that she was going to bed before her husband came looking for her. Nora followed her to the living room where they chatted for another while. When the woman had gone to bed Nora took a good look at the photos on the wall. She took two photographs and put them inside the handbag the woman had given her. She took them because she did not know how to ask the couple to give her the photos. Nora was beginning to suspect something but she feared it might be mere coincidence.

Early the next morning Chris dropped Nora to the nearest bus station, as he has to be early to work. Nora then took a bus to Jane's house. When she arrived she did not see anyone in the house, but the home help told her that Jane had gone out with Tom and the children, while Larry was gone to work, so Nora went to see her father. She returned to Jane's house late in the evening and met Larry, who told her that Jane had gone out with her father and all the children to see one of their neighbours. Nora held Larry's hand and took him upstairs to Tom's room and quickly brought out the photos she had taken from the couple's house. She said: "Larry, take a good look at these photos and tell me what you think."

Larry took the pictures from Nora, looked at them. "This is Tom when he was young," he said, "and this is his brother, this is his sister and this is his father. Where did you get these photos?" he asked.

"I stole them," said Nora.

"You stole them!" Larry said anxiously.

"Yes, I stole them," Nora repeated.

"Why, how, where and when?" asked Larry.

"Larry, it's a very long story but we must work on these photos and when we are through we will tell Tom and Jane, but for now let us keep it a secret. I want you to promise me that you are not going to tell Tom or Jane," Nora demanded.

"Okay, I promise I will not discuss anything with Tom, but as for Jane, it is difficult for me to keep it from her because, if we have to go out, you know she will want an explanation and it would be wrong of me to tell her lies, so I think it is impossible for me not to tell Jane. I suggest we tell Jane and leave Tom out of it. But, tell me, what kept you and where is your car?" Larry asked.

Nora took a deep breath and hissed.

Immediately the bell rang and Larry said that must be Jane and her father with the children. "I must open the door for them," Larry said as he ran downstairs.

They were all very happy to see Nora and Tom shouted with excitement: "Where were you, missing lady?"

They all laughed and Larry said: "Nora just appeared like a ghost when I was about going to the bathroom."

It was like a mission impossible to get Nora to tell them what had happened to her. At one o'clock in the morning, in the stillness of the night, Nora went downstairs at the back of the house and broke down in tears, crying and saying: "Out of the ashes of my dying today I see a brand new day, it is the breaking of a new day and a new hope."

Nora's lamentations woke Jane up. Larry was fast asleep but Jane woke him saying: "Larry! Larry, listen, do you hear anything?"

Larry first said that he did not, but Jane told him to wipe his eyes and listen carefully. In less than a second Larry raised his voice saying: "Oh yes! I can hear it, it sounds sorrowful."

Jane used her hand to close his mouth and told him to lower his voice, that he might wake Tom and the children.

"Oh God, I can feel the vibration of the voice of whoever it is. Let us go and find out," Larry said.

Larry told Jane to stay in bed while he went looking for the source of the sound.

"That is Nora's voice. I must go with you," said Jane, and the two of them started in the direction of the echo.

Larry said the echo of the person's voice was all over the whole house and Jane said it sounded like the echo of a troubled soul.

Then Larry said: "You are not very far from the truth, Jane, someone somewhere certainly is in trouble, but the question still remains who, and where is the voice coming from?"

"The voice is like that of Nora but what could be the problem? Where is she and why would she go out of her room at this hour?" Jane asked worriedly.

"I don't think it is Nora's voice, I did not hear any footsteps, at least I would have heard her footsteps if she had gone downstairs," Larry said.

"How could you have heard, when you were fast asleep? Was I not the one that woke you up?" asked Jane.

They continued arguing in this manner until Larry suggested they check first to see if Nora was in her room, before going any further. They went to her room and found the children sleeping but Nora was not there. It became clear to them then that the voice had to be that of Nora. She was nowhere inside the house so they went outside and saw her sitting down at the back of the house. She was crying floods of tears but they managed to bring her inside. However she would not talk to them but said: "Out of the ashes of my dying today I see the breaking of a brand new day. It is indeed a new day and the mind of the prudent is ever getting knowledge, while the heart of the wise is ever-seeking, enquiring and craving knowledge."

Jane and Larry tried to persuade her to tell them what the problem was, but it was a no-go area. Jane became angry saying:

"Nora, we do not need this iambic pentameter you are creating here. Flying birds twitter and even sluggish streams chatter in appreciation of God's glory, so you should appreciate the fact that, whatever happened, the worst of it is over. You are still alive and I think that even the biggest problem in the world would be solved through dialogue, so talk to us."

Yet Nora did not talk, instead she said: "Every experience in my life brings a change to me and, not only that, it creates knowledge, therefore I would like to be a simple human being with a sincere heart and a serene life which would enable me to overcome all thoughts of discontentment, impurity and self-seeking, because I have seen a new day. I want cheerfulness and humility in my life; I want silence which will lead me to meditation; that, in turn, will bring ideas that command resources because I saw the unimaginable, yet it was real."

Jane, who had already lost her patience, said to Nora: "If you like simplicity then talk to us, spell it out, get out of your shell and free your emotion."

"That is true, there is no other way around it," Larry said.

So Nora began to tell the story of her recent experience: "When I left the hospital I told my father that I was coming straight to you. I had only driven from the hospital and was trying to join the main road when I saw a little boy sitting down by the roadside crying. As soon as I stopped to ask the little boy what was happening to him, a hefty man gave me a pat on the back and told me to go to my car. I thought it was because I had left the car on before I went to the little boy, but when I got to the car I saw another man sitting in the driver's side of the car. They ordered me at gunpoint to get into the car and sit down. I did so and they drove a little distance from the hospital entrance and stopped. Another man got in, a tiny man with dirty teeth who kept smiling and asking me if I was married.

"I did not say anything. They started driving so fast for a very long way and I did not know where I was. They started smoking and one of them asked me if I would like to smoke. I managed to tell them that I neither drank nor smoked. Then another one asked if I was a virgin and he put his hand around my neck. Even though I was drowning in fear, I shouted at him so he became angry and slapped me. I said that my body is a sacred entity and that it is incumbent on me to protect it from every form of contamination. The one driving the car asked, 'And who is contaminating your body?'

"I did not say a word and the next thing that happened was the one sitting beside me started cleaning my face with a white handkerchief containing something like white powder. I immediately pushed his hand away saying, 'Take your filthy hands off me.' Before I knew what was happening one of them gave me another slap; it was as if my mouth was sealed, I couldn't shout, I couldn't cry. I'm not used to praying but I prayed in my heart and I heard a loud cry from my spirit, 'Oh God!' And my mouth never opened.

"A car that was going the opposite direction reversed and followed us. When they discovered that the car was coming after them they slowed down a little and pushed me out with my hands tied at the back and drove away. The man that was chasing after them quickly stopped and came to me. He tried to help me but I refused because, at that particular time, I could not trust anybody, moreover, I had not recovered from the shock and I noticed that the place was very isolated. I refused to tell the man anything because I was still in shock. Later the man left but he came back again and told me to leave that place before I experienced something worse; so I started running. After running a very long distance I ended up in the same man's house. That was where I got those photos; those photos dried my tears and gave me a new hope and a new adventure, so Jane, Larry, this is my story and experience," said Nora.

Jane and Larry were so shocked that they could not talk for about five minutes. Jane brought a glass of water to Nora. "It is like you went to hell, Nora," Larry said.

"That is the only way to describe it because the pangs of death surrounded me and the sneers of hell encompassed me," answered Nora.

"Thank God you are back," said Jane. "Thanks to that man also because if it were not for him, who knows - you might have been history by now," Larry suggested.

"That man is a very nice man and his wife is also very nice. They have three lovely children - Henry, Tommie and Jane - the youngest one is fourteen. I became very interested in the family when I heard the names of the children. I told their mother that the world is so deep, yet very small. By the way what do you think of those names?" asked Nora.

"I think it's a kind of coincidence because remember my father said his only brother's name is Henry, his sister's name is Jane, I am Jane too, and my father is Tom. It is very surprising. Maybe we should try and get close to that family, or what do you feel?" asked Jane.

"That was the reason I took those photos. I know that the couple must think that I am an irresponsible woman. They helped me and the only way I paid them back was by stealing their photos. I pray they will see the reason why they have to forgive my action. We are going on an adventure with those photos and by the time we finish, that couple will be happy but, for now, I think the fact that I took those pictures will be causing problems in that family," said Nora.

"That is a good reason why we have to act fast," Larry said.

"Ah, what are you saying?" asked Jane. "And what do you mean by acting fast? I'm lost here in the middle - can somebody give me an explanation?" Jane demanded.

"Oh, Nora brought some family pictures from the couple that harboured her during her dilemma. I think they have a close connection with Tom because the man himself looks very like Tom and Nora even said that he has your family birthmark, as do his children. The man said the birthmark originated from his grandfather and, according to Nora, the birthmark is exactly like yours and Tom's. It is in the same position so you can see a sort of genetic connection there; that is why she stole the photos, to show us the similarities. I have seen the photos and I did not hesitate to tell Nora that they are your family." Larry moved towards Jane, put his hand around her neck saying: "I know Tom is your father and I know how much you love him but, do not tell him until we are certain that they are your relatives," he pleaded with Jane.

"Where are the photos, please, I want to see them," Jane appealed to Larry and Nora.

They went upstairs. Tom and the children were still asleep. Nora gave the photos to Jane and Jane was astonished. The next day the three of them, Larry Jane and Nora, set out on the quest of tracing the couple.

CHAPTER SEVEN

Time to Say Goodbye

Although Nora was unable to give an accurate description of the way to the area where the couple lived, Larry was convinced that even the most basic description of the road to their place would get them there, provided Nora would be able to locate their house; and so they went on what Nora termed the 'journey of the unknown'. Before they left that morning Tom was suspicious as to why the three of them were going out at the same time and on a weekend, and why they brought another babysitter to mind the children, in addition to the usual babysitter who was there. He asked them but all his efforts to get a reliable answer failed. When they left Tom asked the babysitters whether they had told them where they were going. The babysitters told Tom that they had no idea where they were going and that they only told them to look after the children.

It took about three hours to get to the Christopher's house, with stoppages and other delays. When they got there, Nora stayed in the car while Jane and Larry went up to the house. They met the couple who received them with open arms; but as soon as Larry made mention of a woman they had helped some days back, the expression on Chris's wife face turned to one of anger and disappointment, and her husband asked them whether they knew the woman. Larry said that they did and Chris asked Larry how he could make contact with the woman because she had something belonging to them. Larry told them that they did not need to worry about the woman, that she did not mean any harm. Then Chris's wife said that such an act was not good, that it did not speak well of her and that they were still wondering what her intention was by taking photos of people she did not know. She was very angry and was still trying to talk when her husband told her to keep quiet.

Then her husband asked Larry how he could make contact with the woman. Larry repeated to him that he did not need to, that they had the photos with them. He brought out the photos and gave them to Chris, who exchanged a surprised look with his wife.

Jane said: "She is my friend, my best friend, and she is right here."

She went outside and brought Nora in. Chris stood up and his wife hissed and went away. Chris asked Nora to sit down, which she did while apologizing for her actions. Larry laughed and said that there was no need for an apology; that Nora had done what she did in Chris' interest and that of the entire family. Chris wanted to talk but Larry stopped him, saying that they had forgotten the most important thing. Chris asked him what he meant.

"Oh, it is simple - the introduction," said Jane.

"Yes, we did not even bother with the introduction. My name is Larry and this is Jane, my dear wife. And this lady you already know is Nora, my wife's best friend."

"Oh, that is interesting," said Chris, "my daughter's name is Jane as well and my own name is Chris, the short form of Christopher."

"Ah, what a nice name, and my grandfather's name is Christopher too," said Jane.

"Ah ha, that is another co-incidence; my own grandfather's name is Christopher too. I was named after him" said Chris. Jane turned and looked at Nora and Larry and they all smiled.

"This is just the beginning; many more surprises are on the way - I was named after my grandmother too," Jane said.

"My daughter was named after my grandmother too," said Chris, "my grandmother's name is Jane, but she is no more."

"My grandmother too is no more, although I never saw her, but my father told me so much about her," Jane said.

Jane asked him to bring the pictures they had given back to him earlier. Chris asked his wife to bring the photos. Jane picked out three different pictures and asked Chris if he could identify the people in the photos. He quickly said to Jane: "This is my mother and her two brothers and these are my grandparents. My mother told me who they all were before she died and, according to her, they are all late. My mother was named after her mother."

"Well, you are right and wrong at the same time, because right now, as I speak with you, one of them is still alive and he will be very happy to see you," said Jane.

"This discussion is taking a very complicated dimension; please, can someone get straight to the point and tell me what is happening, because this whole thing is becoming a mirage to me?" Chris said.

The anxiety in his face was mounting, but Jane told him to calm down, that all would be unfolded shortly. Larry told Chris to tell them about his mother. Chris told them the story of how his mother was married to a man who he described as 'mysterious' when she was very young. It was a polygamous family and not just that, he said, because of strange things that were happening there, his mother ran away, not knowing that she was pregnant. "She was lucky because an elderly woman who I thought was my grandmother took care of her. She is also late, but I learned my mother was almost dead when she met that elderly woman who totally transformed her, according to my mother. Anyway thanks to God, I met her and showed her my love and appreciation for what she did for my mother," Chris explained.

"Transformation is one of the world's biggest processes, because the only thing that does not change in this world is change itself. I think we know your story very well, if not more than yourself, but can you call the children as we want to see them, please?" Jane requested gently.

"Why not," said Chris, who quickly went and brought the children. The oldest boy was wearing a pair of shorts and a vest and Nora and Jane looked knowingly at one another. Jane went to him saying: "You are very tall, like my father." She touched him, smiled, and said: "Oh, I like your birthmark."

"I have one too and every one of them has it," said Chris, "it is from my mother, as I told you before."

"Oh yes, I know. I saw it when I slept in your house, that was what pushed me to take those photos," Nora said.

Nora whispered to Jane to pull up her sleeve and show them her own birthmark, but Jane told her that she wanted to see

Chris' birthmark first. Jane and Nora asked the second son to remove his shirt because they want to see his birthmark, while Jane helped his daughter to pull her sleeve up. When Chris removed his shirt, Jane pulled her sleeve up. Larry laughed and started clapping, saying: "This is a festival of birthmarks."

Chris' wife was petrified and Chris himself was speechless. Jane started crying saying: "I was born to die, I was thrown away like a piece of rubbish and somebody picked me up and gave me life and hope. In the midst of my happiness, I lost her, but before she died she told me the truth about my identity. I wished I had not been born and when she died I thought it was the end of the world. Nora lifted me up from the land of lost hope. Nobody knew my identity. Throughout my time at university they thought Nora was my sister. I found my father and today my eyes have seen the unimaginable - this is a miracle." Jane turned and hugged Chris' daughter, holding her tightly and crying while saying in a loud voice: "Today, another big story has been added to the annals of my life."

Larry moved to Jane and hugged her. Smiling he said: "This is just the beginning. Greater things are coming. The days of tears, agony and sorrow are gone and it is a new day indeed." He turned to Chris and said: "Chris, this is Jane, your cousin."

Chris moved forward and hugged Jane, and he was crying too. Jane, Chris, his wife, little Jane, all of them were crying. Larry stood up and shouted: "Hip-hip hooray! Hip-hip hooray! It is no longer a festival of birthmarks but a festival of tears." All of them started laughing.

Nora reminded Larry and Jane that they had to go home and see to their children and Tom, and to prepare dinner. A very happy Chris told his wife to pack both the food she had cooked and some suitcases as they were going with Larry, Jane and Nora to see Tom. He added that they could all eat together when they got there.

"You did not even ask whether we had a good house like yours," said Larry.

"Even if it is a pit, we are all going to sleep there tonight. I can't wait to see my mother's youngest brother, whom she never stopped talking about. Even when she was dying my mother mentioned her brothers, and especially her youngest brother,"

Chris said as he moved towards Nora, hugged her, but did not know what to tell her; all he managed to say through his tears was: "You are a saint. I'm sorry."

The entire group left together to see Tom. When they got there it was already dark and Tom was worried about their whereabouts. He complained to the babysitters that they had never done such a thing before. Suddenly the doorbell rang and one of the babysitters opened the door and Jane came in. While the babysitter complained to Nora and Larry that Tom had not eaten anything, because he had been worried about them, Jane ran to Tom and told him that they had good news, but that he had to promise that he would eat before they broke the news. Tom, however, insisted that he must hear the news before he ate. But Jane refused and said that he must eat before getting the news. While they argued, Larry, Christopher and the others brought provisions out from the car boots.

Larry came in with some suitcases and overheard Jane and Tom still arguing. Larry said: "Oh no, Tom, no food, no good news. Do we have a deal here, Dad?"

"Yes, it is a promise," said Tom.

Jane brought his food and as he was eating Chris and his family came in. Tom thought they were Nora's sisters and brothers, so he just said: "You have a battalion here."

"Yes, and those battalions are going to sleep with us here tonight," said Jane.

"Pretty good," Tom responded and continued eating his food.

When the babysitters left everybody gathered together to eat, and encouraged Tom to eat some of the food they had brought from Chris' house. When they had finished eating Larry brought all the children together and they all sat down around Tom. Larry asked Tom to tell them a story, as was usual, before they go to bed.

Tom wanted to tell them the story of a limping barber, but Jane said: "We have heard that story several times, we want a new story."

Tom told them the story of an orphan whose foster mother abused him mentally, physically and emotionally. She never called him by his name, not even once, she used to call him 'Big Head'. When the boy grew up and saved the woman from certain death she was in deep sorrow because of what she had done to the boy all those years back. "She never knew that it is only time that decides every situation," said Tom.

Everyone was quiet after Tom's story, so he asked his listeners what they had learned. He insisted that each of them give their answers, one by one, including the children. They all gave their answers, after which Tom commented that they all gave the right answers.

"But listen to me, all of you," Tom continued, "the most important lesson here is that no human is more important than the other. He who is a child will certainly become an adult one day, and freedom is the right of all humanity. Moreover, he who is holding the key today may not have it tomorrow, because tomorrow is pregnant and no one knows what it is going to deliver. Finally, always bear in mind that nobody is indispensable, myself included," Tom concluded.

"My mom called me a pig when she threw me into the dump and she also called that woman that nursed me a pig," Jane said.

"Enough of that, Jane!" Nora interrupted her, "you only knew that she called you a pig because that lady told you."

"She called me a pig too but that did not matter to me," said Tom.

"Anyway, that pig that was thrown away like a piece of rubbish now belongs to a family," Larry said.

Larry looked at Chris, who was eagerly waiting to be introduced to Tom. Larry got the message promptly and told Tom that it was time for the good news. He started with Chris, asking him to stand up in front of Tom. Chris stood up and Larry told Tom to take a good look at the man in front of him and tell him what he thought about him. Tom looked at Chris several times and then said: "He is a very tall and good-looking man."

"Okay, let us move to another stage - Chris, remove your shirt," Larry said.

Chris removed his shirt and Tom said: "Oh, he has a birthmark like me."

Then Larry said: "Stage Three: Chris, tell your family to introduce themselves."

Chris and his family said their names. Tom was motionless after hearing their names and he repeated their surname three times.

"What is so special about their surname, Dad, that you are still mentioning it?" Larry asked Tom.

"I was just thinking about other things," Tom stammered.

"What other things are you thinking about, Dad?" asked Larry.

"Oh, I like their names," said Tom, still looking at Chris.

"Why do you like their names?" Larry asked.

"I like them because my father's name is Christopher, my brother's name is Henry, and my sister's name is Jane," Tom replied.

Larry told the boys to remove their shirts and the girl to pull up her sleeve, and for Jane to do likewise. They all did as Larry told them to do. When Tom saw their birthmarks he jumped up saying: "Jesus! Jesus Christ! Who are these people and why are they here?"

Larry moved to Tom, put his hand around his neck and said: "Tom, we have found your sister but unfortunately she died a few months ago: this is her son and these are his children, your nephews and niece, and this is his wife, so you have a full house and a large family."

Tom jumped up for joy saying: "It is not where we are today that matters, but where we are going to be tomorrow. Our going is important but our arrival is more important. Look at the clock, it ticks non-stop. Time, it is only time that heals a wound. My tears of yesteryear are gone for my eyes have seen a miracle."

When Tom finished talking, he cried in a loud voice, saying: "That my father is alive today, that my mother is alive today, that my brother is alive today, that my sister is alive today, the sky should have been my limit. Oh death, the enemy of mankind, why should you be, must you be?"

Tom continued crying while Chris and Larry were holding and consoling him. The echo of his voice carried throughout the whole house and at the same time Nora and Jane echoed a very loud cry. Larry looked at them and said: "Oh these are the echoes of troubled souls or, no, the echoes of joyful souls."

"Or rather the echo of a united family," Chris suggested.

Jane looked at the clock and said to Tom that it was time to go to bed.

"No, not today," Tom replied.

Chris and his family stayed at Tom's house, while Nora left the next day with her children. Jane, Larry and their children stayed in the house while Tom went to spend time at Chris' home and visit his sister's grave. After a week, Tom came back. He told Larry and Jane about everything that his sister had gone through, as he had been told by his sister's son. From that moment onwards Chris' family - Tom, Larry, Jane and their children - exchanged visits and sleepovers, and they were regularly with one another.

One night, after the celebration of Larry's birthday, when the whole family had gathered again including Nora and her children, they sat around Tom and asked him to tell them a story as usual before they went to bed. Surprisingly, Tom said no, that they should tell him a story instead; that over the years he had been the one telling the stories and that it was their turn to tell the story while he listened. He pointed to Chris and told him to tell a story.

Larry asked Tom why the sudden change of mind, Tom said: "Because I might not be here tomorrow to tell you a story, so you have to do it yourselves, because someone must fill that vacuum in case anything happens. I'm not going to live forever, that is certain, and you all know that."

Tom continued: "You must always be ready for every eventuality and watch out for danger, because the world itself is turning into a dangerous place to live in, and we must make time for everything - time to make merry and time for sadness, they are all part of human activities; finally, there is a time to live and a time to say goodbye, either temporarily or permanently."

Larry was confused on hearing Tom's statement and Jane was afraid, so they asked him whether he was going somewhere and what had made him say those things, that they had never heard such statements from him before. Tom laughed and said that they would not understand, but that it would be clear to them in future days. Then the anxious Larry asked him whether he had seen a vision. Tom did not respond but just laughed and asked

Chris to tell a story. Chris told a story and afterwards Tom asked Chris' wife to tell a story, which she did also. After hearing her story, they all thought they were going to bed, but Tom shouted: "Who's next?"

Larry said it was his turn and when he had finished telling his story Jane knew that it was her turn to tell a story. After Jane Nora did not wait, but duly told her own story. Then Tom said: "Oh yes, mission accomplished."

Larry stood up in a disturbed manner saying: "Wait, wait, and wait! Something strange is going on here, Dad, what mission is accomplished?"

Tom laughed and said: "Do this every night, not just in this house, but in your various houses. You must pass it on, not just to your children, but to the generation that is to come after you. Always wear knowledge like a wristwatch: bring it out when you need it because, when you stop learning, you will start dying. Be permanent students in the school of your spirits because if you stop learning you will start dying, I repeat. I have said these things before and you all have heard it before."

They were all confused and pondering Tom's words, and Tom asked Larry and Chris to bring a mattress outside the house and put it in front of the mango tree. They did so and he told them to climb the mango tree; that they should go high up, one after another and let themselves fall down; that he was going to catch them so that they would not get injured. Larry was afraid that he was going to injure Tom when he fell into his hands so he said: "Are you not too old for this kind of task, Dad?"

"I wonder if we should be the ones doing that for him because his bones are weak and he is full of age," Chris said.

Larry knelt down before Tom, pleading with him that they should do something else. Tom insisted that they do it and laughed, saying: "I know that you are youths and I am old; you are young and hot blood runs through your veins; but I am going to prove to you that this old man you see here is still pretty much mentally alive."

"We know that, Dad, but we are worried about your physical competence for this task," Larry said.

Tom laughed and said to them: "Exuberance is the prerogative of youths, while wisdom is a virtue of age." Tom repeated that he was going to catch them in his hands and that they were not going to fall onto the mattress at all. Larry went first and left himself fall. Tom moved and Larry fell on top of the mattress. Chris was laughing looking at Larry and Tom himself was laughing too.

"Dad, you said you were going to carry me in your hands," laughed Larry.

"Oh, I was looking elsewhere, I'm sorry," said Tom.

Chris was standing beside Tom, laughing, and Tom asked him: "What are you waiting for?"

"I'm waiting for you to tell me to climb the tree, uncle," answered Chris.

"Go on so, do it then," Tom replied.

Chris climbed the mango tree and Tom did the same thing that he had done to Larry. Larry started laughing and Tom laughed too, saying: "Never trust anybody, not even myself, no matter how long we live. Life is too short and it is easier to forgive than to take the path of revenge. Be of good courage all the time, embrace wisdom, make understanding your next-of-kin and always remember to be there for one another."

Larry was about to ask a question but Tom said: "Too late, it is time to go to bed and time to say goodbye and good night."

They went inside and Tom went and touched all the children and went to his room. Larry, Jane and Chris wanted to ask Tom the meaning of what he had said, but he told them that he was weak and needed to go to bed and answer the call of nature. So they left him and went to bed.

Later in the night Jane woke with a loud cry, saying that she had had a terrible nightmare. The next day, very early in the morning, Larry went to Tom's room only to discover that Tom was dead. Larry wept and said in a loud voice: "We are like writing pencils in the eyes of the almighty, and he can clean us up whenever it pleases him."